The Body in the Vat

Tales from the Tannery

An Old Bethlehem Mystery

Charlene Donchez Mowers

Carol A. Reifinger

Charlene Donchez Mowers

Carol A. Reifinger

The Body in the Vat is a work of fiction.
All of the characters and events in the book are fictitious.
The places mentioned are real, but their descriptions
are not meant to be exact.

ISBN 978-0-692-32129-4

Cover photos by Linda Wickmann
Graphic design by Sandy Yoder

Printed in the United States of America
Christmas City Printing
November 2014
Bethlehem, Pennsylvania

TABLE OF CONTENTS

Acknowledgements

Prologue   A Young Soldier's Dilemma - *October 12, 1862*

A Glossary of Moravian Terms

Appendices:
    Historic Bethlehem Museums & Sites
    Historic Moravian Bethlehem
    Central Moravian Church
    The Moravian Denomination
    The Old Chapel
    Moravian Archives
    Bethlehem Area Moravians, Inc.
    For Further Reading

W<small>E</small> gratefully acknowledge the encouragement and support of a number of Bethlehem people and organizations. Central Moravian Church Pastors, the Rt. Rev. C. Hopeton Clennon and the Rev. Janel R. Rice, have cheered us on our way and we are appreciative.

The Board of Trustees of Historic Bethlehem Museums & Sites has graciously given us permission to share as backdrop some of the wonderful old buildings still standing in historic Bethlehem, especially the 1761 Tannery and the 1869 Luckenbach Mill in the Colonial Industrial Quarter.

Many thanks to David Roth, General Manager of Bethlehem Area Moravians, Inc., for allowing us to describe a bit about the meaningful work of "BAM" in the community.

Dr. Paul Peucker has been invaluable in providing historical background information and a description of the workings of the Moravian Archives in his role as Archivist. Assistant Archivist Tom McCullough researched some of the early plans of the Tannery for us. We thank them both for their help.

We want to thank Bruce Haines of the Historic Hotel Bethlehem, Dana Devito, Manager of the Moravian Book Shop and Patti Sakdiponephong, owner of the Café, for their support and good wishes for the success of our book.

Photographer Linda Wickmann worked diligently to capture an especially foreboding view of the Tannery. We thank her for her persistence in getting just the right feel for the photos that appear on the front and back covers of the book.

Graphic designer Sandy Yoder has been a real gift to us and a steadfast encourager. Thank you!

To our spouses, George Mowers and Jim Reifinger, we offer our sincere and loving thanks for your forbearance and advice. You helped us to enter the challenging world of fiction writing and from the start, encouraged us to write our *next* mystery.

The proceeds from the sale of this book will be shared with Historic Bethlehem Museums & Sites and the 275th Anniversary Committee of Moravians in Bethlehem.

The Body in the Vat

Tales from the Tannery

Bethlehem, Pennsylvania
Sunday, October 12, 1862

The young soldier pulled the tin box under his arm as tightly as he could against his body. Frantically, he looked from side to side as his eyes became accustomed to the pitch dark of the old Tannery. In the room to his left, he could just make out the outline of the large, square vats, filled with the black dregs of tanning liquid and water. Scanning the walls behind the vats, he could not see a hiding place for the box. So he turned back toward the large entry room with its open wooden steps and landing leading to the second floor.

A small ray of light from under the upstairs door revealed a bulge in the old stone wall near the top of the steps. Carefully, he knelt down and tapped against the loose stone, edging it away from the wall. The stone broke loose. There behind it was an opening large enough to slide in the tin box.

Just as he pounded the stone back in to cover the box, he heard the sound of the back door inside the next room creaking open. Suddenly, he heard the rushing water of the creek from behind the building and then the gravelly scraping of heavy boots moving across the stone floor of the Tannery. Sweat rolled down his face from under his blue cap. The smell of his damp woolen uniform mingled with the odor of the tanning fluid, making him nauseous. In the distance he could hear the old bell of Central Church clanging the hour.

His heart pounded as the footsteps came closer. Suddenly, the door to the hall swung open and a shot exploded at his head. He jumped from the landing and ran toward the vats. He panicked and looked for a place to escape. His last thoughts were of the young woman who loved him and the child he would never see.

CHAPTER ONE

"A Dark and Stormy Night"

ADELE glanced at the clock on her desk and then out the window and realized that it wasn't just getting to be evening, but the skies had darkened with storm clouds. Since her husband, Zeke, was playing basketball this evening at a local high school gym, she decided to stay and get some work done at the office tonight.

The storm had better not set off the office building's security alarm, she thought in a brief panic. Not that security was the issue, it was the alarm that fed into the police department that concerned her. Another false alarm going off would be really annoying and disruptive, not to mention the police false alarm charge. She wanted peace and quiet this evening to get something done.

Picking up the phone, she decided to call Mitzi at the Old Mill.

"Your husband told me that I'd find you there," Adele said into the phone tucked under her chin.

She was stacking up some paperwork as she stood looking out at the dark skies and the rain pounding hard against her second floor window in the Church office building. Her normally cozy, cheerful office was almost gloomy tonight. The deep red oriental carpet on the floor seemed to absorb every bit of light that the small table lamp shed across her mahogany desk.

"You found me," Mitzi said. "Vaughn just called and told me that the storm is strengthening. I thought I'd check for any imminent flooding and maybe put the police on the alert."

Mitzi was the head of the Bethlehem Historical Society and had her office in the Old Mill, infamous for getting flooded on a regular basis, before the dam was removed just a year ago. More than once, rowboats had to come in and rescue nearby residents of the old Moravian Industrial Quarter. Because flooding was a now familiar scenario, Mitzi was fairly unconcerned about the storm this evening, trusting that it would blow over without too much damage to the buildings and grounds.

"Just don't get caught in it yourself," Adele cautioned Mitzi. "I won't keep you, but I wanted to give you a quick update on our program."

Adele had served the venerable old Central Moravian Church as a pastor for the last 25 years and in more recent times, as Senior Pastor. For years, the Church and the Society had been working closely together. It made a lot of sense for both institutions. This time they were teaming up for "Moravian Days," a festival on the sprawling Church Green, part of which they shared with the Moravian Museum, one of the historic sites of the Society. It was a complicated organization, but it worked. The fact that she and Mitzi were friends helped to add energy to Moravian Days planning.

"What's going on? Are the dates we wanted still ok?" Mitzi asked hopefully. "I certainly…" and then her voice suddenly trailed off.

Silence. Something was definitely wrong.

"Mitzi?"

"Uh, there appears to be a man standing under the light on the pole at the corner of the parking lot. He's staring right in this direction. Good heavens, what is he doing out there in the pouring rain?" responded Mitzi with a hint of trepidation in her voice.

He was wearing a green slicker raincoat with a hood. It almost looked like he was holding a gun at his side, protecting it from the rain. That can't be possible, she thought. She must be seeing things.

Tourists who wandered around the historic Moravian buildings were determined to see what the area had to offer, rain or shine. But this was ridiculous. Adele hoped that perhaps Mitzi would recognize the man as an office worker, or even one of the grounds keepers.

"Never saw him before," Mitzi said. "He's just standing there. It's a little crazy. There's such a downpour out there…"

"Don't you think you should call the police?" Adele asked, recognizing a decided edge in her friend's voice, very uncharacteristic of her.

Mitzi always seemed so self-confident and decisive. She was someone who wasn't intimidated by much: not by quarrelsome Board members, not City Hall, not anything. But this situation was strange and unsettling.

"Adele, I just turned away for a moment and now he's gone! I think I hear someone rattling the door downstairs. I don't really feel comfortable letting someone in at this hour." It was well after 7 pm and no one would venture out on an evening like this.

"Don't do it! Look, get off the phone and then call the police. Don't try to win any medals for bravery, girl."

"I'll listen for a minute and then give Vaughn a call to come and meet me. I'm not going out to my car alone."

For a moment, Adele imagined Mitzi's husband Vaughn driving through the storm in his low slung, silver sports car. Would he even be able to get through any flooded roads near the Mill?

"Do it right now. Call me back if you need me. I'm going to stay put for a while."

When Adele hung up, she looked out at the storm and the trees being whipped by the wind and then decided to drive down there herself. Maybe she could convince her friend to leave.

The Mill was just a two minute trip down the hill. She gathered her briefcase and purse and dashed downstairs. No one else was in the building, so she pulled her umbrella from the antique blue and white porcelain stand, set the alarm and turned out the foyer light. She hurried along the sidewalk to the gate leading to the parking lot. In just the short time it took to cross the lot and get into the car, she was soaked from the steady downpour.

Thinking that she'd approach the Mill parking lot from the creek side, she drove around the large parking lot under the Hill-to-Hill Bridge and cautiously made her way over the old, one lane, stone-arched bridge, glancing at the creek on both sides and hoping that she would not get trapped by the rising water.

The windshield wipers struggled to keep up with the deluge. It was really impossible to see the road.

As she pulled into the apparently empty lot, she saw Mitzi's small black car, but there was no one standing in the rain.

She got out of her car, sloshing in a puddle as she went. She popped open her umbrella against the wind and dashed across the lot to the Mill door and yelled up to Mitzi's window, "Mitzi, it's me. Let me in!"

No one answered. The Old Mill looked especially foreboding tonight because the office windows on the first floor were completely dark, but a pale yellow light was still shining out into the parking lot from Mitzi's office on the second floor. Adele had a queasy feeling that she and Mitzi should get out of there soon.

CHAPTER TWO

Intruder at the Door

AFTER she hung up with Adele, Mitzi slowly made her way down the shadowy stairs of the Mill. The lighting in the old building was kept dim purposely so that paintings and artifacts would be protected. But on a night like this, the low lighting gave a sinister look to the hallways.

She continued to hear rattling at the rough wooden door at the bottom of the far landing.

Her mind was racing as she took a few hesitant steps closer to the door. Who would be out in this terrible storm? Is he in need of help? Is he a lost tourist trying to find his way back to the Hotel Bethlehem? He could be…well, she didn't want to think about that. In all these 14 years at the museum, she had many weird experiences, but this was the first time that she ever felt truly frightened.

She could still hear Adele's voice only moments ago at the other end of the phone telling her to get out. Maybe she should have called the police, at least.

Standing close to the door, she called out firmly, "Who is it? What do you want?"

There was no response, but the rattling suddenly stopped. All she heard was the beating of the rain against the walls and door.

She was not about to open the door. Instead, she quickly made her way back up to her office and the telephone. The wind was getting stronger now and beginning to howl. So many nights she had worked late and never been bothered. Why tonight? And now apparently, she'd lost track of the strange interloper outside stalking her.

Worried about her own safety, as well as Mitzi's, Adele ran back to her car and decided to call Mitzi on her cell phone. Startled by the sound of her cell phone ringing just as she started to pick up the desk phone,

Mitzi answered, "Adele, thank goodness it's you! I was just about to call the police. I lost track of the man. He was trying to get in here! Where are you?"

"I'm right outside in the parking lot. Didn't you hear me banging on the door?"

"No, I thought it was the man! But why are you here? You were at the door? You got out of your car? With that man stalking around? Didn't you just tell me to be careful?"

"I was worried. So come down and let me in until the police come."

"I'll be right down, but be careful with that man lurking around the building."

Just as Adele got out of her car and started for the Mill door, Mitzi looked out the window and saw the stranger coming around the other side of the building. She raced downstairs to let Adele in, but the old wooden door was stuck... badly warped from all the dampness. Mitzi pushed from the inside. Adele pulled on the old iron handle from the outside. As the rain continued to pour down the side of the building, the wind slammed against the Mill in gusts.

Mitzi yelled out, "Adele, he is headed this way! Pull!"

Finally, the door opened with a *whoosh* and Adele fell backward onto the porch floor. Mitzi yelled above the wind, "Get up! Get in here!"

She grabbed her friend's hand and pulled her inside. The door slammed shut. They bolted it before racing up the stairs to the safety of Mitzi's office.

Mitzi immediately call the police. A polite young officer answered. "Yes ma'am, we'll try to get to you as soon as we can, but there are wires down all over town and the creek is starting to overrun its banks. Keep the doors locked and stay inside."

All of a sudden they heard a loud crack and then a crashing noise coming from inside. The lights in the building flickered and went out. They were alone, without power in the 150 year-old Mill.

CHAPTER THREE

Police Report

REACTING quickly, Mitzi said firmly, feeling her way in the dark, "Okay, we need to see what that was."

She pulled out a bottom desk drawer and rummaged around for a flashlight. "It almost sounds like something came through a window somewhere down the hall."

"Right behind you," Adele said, arming herself with her soaking wet pink umbrella, a bizarre looking weapon of self-defense, to be sure. "You lead the way. You know this old building."

Finding their way was tricky, with just the flashlight to illuminate the dark hallways, but finally they got to the door to the room that they suspected had been hit.

As they opened the door, a sudden, cold burst of air brushed against their faces. They could see that a window directly across from them was smashed to pieces. There in the circle of light from the flashlight lay a pile of broken glass and a part of a limb from the old willow tree that stood next to the Mill.

They stepped closer to the window and could see the headlights of Vaughn's car pulling into the deserted lot.

"It's a good thing you called Vaughn," said Adele.

"No, I didn't! I never had the chance. And let's not tell him about the man in the slicker."

Adele insisted, "No, Vaughn has to know!"

Vaughn was concerned about Mitzi working late at the Old Mill by herself, with this storm. Driving over the bridge, he knew that he was right to come down. All the lights were out and he could see the flicker of a flashlight in an upper floor window.

Mitzi and Adele made their way back downstairs and let him in and quickly told their story.

With Vaughn's help, they covered the window with one of the blue tarps set aside for the upcoming Blueberry Festival in July, and then pushed an old metal cabinet against the broken window.

As Mitzi locked the building securely, she promised Adele that she would file a police report first thing in the morning. Adele promised Mitzi that she would give her husband Zeke a call once she got up to Main Street. With a sigh of relief, they hugged and left the rapidly flooding parking lot at the same time.

Vaughn followed Mitzi and Adele as they drove in a slowly moving caravan over the one lane, stone-arched bridge to higher ground and safety. As he looked back at the Mill in his rear view mirror, he couldn't help but wonder what possible evidence the police would ever find tomorrow after all this wind and rain and slowly rising creek water.

In a few hours, the rain tapered off and stopped. As the clouds blew away across the dark skies, the moon appeared over the old Moravian buildings near the creek, lighting the imposing old Luckenbach Mill, the 1762 Waterworks and the 1761 Tannery. Silent sentinels in the pale moonlight, they guarded their secrets behind sturdy fieldstone walls as the swollen creek rushed by.

The next day was so brilliantly sunny and windy that it was hard to imagine the fury of the storm the previous night. Except for some scattered branches on the sidewalks, most of Bethlehem's streets were clear and unscathed. The traffic lights that were blinking yellow last night had been repaired and the day's activities began again as normal.

From their home set on a hill, Mitzi and Vaughn could see clearly from their kitchen window that the low lying areas were flooded. The creek spilled its banks once again, but not so badly as to damage any of her buildings in the Industrial Quarter.

Resigned to the fact that there was nothing she and her staff could do at the Mill until the water subsided, Mitzi cleared the breakfast dishes, kissed Vaughn goodbye and drove to City Hall to make a police report about the stranger she encountered the night before.

Bethlehem's City Hall was a nondescript gray building set off to the side of a large plaza punctuated by the *Symbol of Progress*, a tall steel sculpture expressing the coming together of the three parts of Bethlehem and reaching skyward, but to some, it actually looked like a celery stalk, stripped down in three sections.

She recalled the stories that Adele told her of visiting an elderly friend who showed her photos of what the area looked like before any of the municipal buildings or plaza were erected. Helen was a feisty little lady who had a long memory and a short fuse. Helen, for one, felt that the whole project was definitely less than an improvement.

Familiar with the City Hall building from her many visits to see the mayor or one of the department heads, Mitzi knew the security routine. Show your ID, sign in at the reception desk and get your name tag and pass.

She was dreading this particular visit, but not as concerned with filing a police report so much as she was concerned about running into a certain local gadfly.

She dearly hoped to avoid another confrontation with Merrill Houser about the tree he wanted to plant in the historic district in honor of his mother. The tree issue was just the latest in a long string of issues that Merrill deposited at her doorstep. It was Merrill who always tried to lobby whatever group he could with his quirky demands.

Probably the real reason that Mitzi hoped to avoid him was that he was always trying to corner her to get her to do personal research for him about his genealogy, convinced that there was a strong Bethlehem connection in his family, going back to at least the time of the Civil War.

It gave her a headache just to think about it. First of all, research on demand was not in her job description and second, even when she had tried to help him in the past, he didn't seem at all satisfied. Without missing a beat, he would turn around and complain to anyone who would listen, about one or another of the Bethlehem Historical Society's sins of commission or omission, depending on the day.

Grudgingly, Mitzi had relented and decided to ask her friend and volunteer, Fred Lang, to help with some genealogy about Merrill's family. Having retired recently from a local corporation as chief engineer, Fred wanted to stay active and was always interested in family stories and doing research. He began digging into some old records at the local historical societies and online to see what he could find out about the Houser family.

As she walked down the grey corridors of City Hall, she pondered whether or not to tell Merrill about any of this. But first, she needed to take care of the police report.

She entered the Police Department and asked to speak to an officer who could take her statement. The young officer dutifully recorded the information, but seemed a bit skeptical when she mentioned that she thought that the stranger in the rain could have had a gun. She saw what she saw. At some point she should mention the gun to Vaughn and Adele, she thought. Would they be skeptical, too?

CHAPTER FOUR

Lunch at Hotel B

JUST before Mitzi was about to leave for her lunch meeting with Adele, Fred Lang came bounding into her office. Fred was a big, lovable character who got so excited when he found juicy tidbits of information. As always, there was a domino effect when he did genealogical work for the Society. One piece of information led to another and another.

"Just wait until you hear what I found out about the Houser family. Merrill's ancestors came to the Easton area from Europe in the 1820's. Taking advantage of the influx of workers who were building the canals along the Delaware and Lehigh Rivers, the Houser clan opened a dry goods store, selling goods to the canal workers and to local residents.

"Later, when the Moravians started selling land in what was to become South Bethlehem in the 1840's, they moved here and eventually opened another store. Once again, they wanted to take advantage of new developments like the zinc company and the Saucona Iron Company, which, as you know, later became the Bethlehem Steel Corporation. Workers needed a place to buy their day-to-day supplies and the Housers were only too happy to comply. They always seemed to be at the right place at the right time. One of Merrill's ancestors also served in the Civil War, but I'll let you know when I find out more details about him."

An interesting sidelight of Fred's research was that the name Mark Sargent popped up. Sargent was a great-great-great grandson of the Union soldier, Private Joe Carver. Carver's name was linked to the Housers', but not in a good way, so Fred was reluctant to tell Mitzi too much more until his research work was finished.

Mitzi had just mentioned Joe Carver's name two weeks ago, when coincidentally, a Mark Sargent contacted her looking for information about Joe's mysterious and sudden demise almost 150 years ago.

Mitzi suggested that Fred spend some time with Elaine Ettwein, who had done a good deal of research on old Bethlehem families. Fred happily agreed to call Elaine, since they had often worked on committees together and had a number of mutual friends.

"I'll give her a call this afternoon," he said, standing to leave. "I'm sure that Elaine can be a great help. Glad you thought of her!"

The Tap Room at Hotel Bethlehem provided a panoramic view of Main Street's small shops, its restaurants with their outdoor tables under dark green umbrellas, its ornate Victorian streetlights and wooden benches with fancy black ironwork.

The early spring day had become warm and sunny, bringing out a noontime parade of office workers, conference goers, shoppers and tourists. Mothers pushed strollers with squirmy children eager to jump out and run along the red brick pavements. College students scuffed along in their flip flops, tee shirts and shorts to classes in the buildings south of Church Street.

Adele's mind wandered as she looked out the window waiting for Mitzi. It was just 10 minutes to 12 and they were supposed to meet at noon. Adele was chronically early for everything. It was a problem at times. A bit on the obsessive compulsive side maybe, she was unable to be late for an appointment of any kind. Being exactly on time meant that she was late.

Although very demanding of herself, being a pastor certainly forced you to be less and less demanding of others, she thought. After 25 years in the ministry, you learned that people were generally well intentioned, even if they didn't, or couldn't, always follow through. Her mind wandered back to a young woman she counseled early in her ministry at Central Church who was so anxious to come and talk but simply didn't show up. She discovered later that the woman's mother had been in a car accident that afternoon and was rushed to a hospital. Adele ended up visiting both of them that evening.

She had to recognize that human beings could not control day to day events. On the other hand, some people did have a knack for making bad decisions about their finances or about their relationships. Sometimes it was a challenge for her to be patient.

Her husband, Zeke always reminded her, "Take the log out of your own eye first." She bristled when his Bible quotations were so *à propos*, but she knew that he was right. Learning to accept her own limitations was a struggle sometimes. She was the type of person who wanted to control a situation rather than be passive. Yet there were some things you couldn't control, no matter how hard you tried.

Thank goodness she had Zeke. Aside from his annoying ability to remind her that she was only human, he was a wonderful husband and advisor. She felt fortunate every day that he was so supportive of her ministry, even if at the time, ministry was an odd career path for a woman.

As Mitzi was walking to the Hotel, she was thinking how lucky she was to have Vaughn as her husband. He was a great guy, always there to encourage her and be her #1 volunteer, ready to help with the behind the scenes details of the Society. Vaughn had retired early, but worked as a financial consultant, with clients all across the Lehigh Valley.

This whole interest in the Civil War, with the Housers and Carvers in the North, made her remember that Vaughn's family on his mother's side lived in South Carolina for generations before the War. She wondered if these families had ever crossed paths during the conflict.

The old bell in the belfry of Central Moravian Church began clanging the noon hour just as Mitzi arrived and pulled out a chair across the table.

"Am I late?" she asked. "I decided to walk over from my meeting, since it was such a nice day outside."

"Not at all," Adele said, shaking her head. "That was scary last night, wasn't it? How is the flooding, by the way?"

"Well, it was just superficial and has already subsided, but it will still take time for us to assess any damage on the grounds. The Tannery and

Waterworks came through unscathed. As far as our scary experience goes, there is something I should really tell you."

"Did the police find the guy?"

"No, not yet, it's just that I could have sworn that he was holding a gun under his slicker when I saw him standing there in the rain."

"What?! Why didn't you tell me this before?"

"At first I wasn't so sure, but then I realized that I had a pretty good look at him. He was standing right under the corner light in the parking lot."

"You did tell the police all of this, I hope."

"Yes, this morning. The officer who took my statement was very nice, but I don't think that he quite believed me."

They talked over the events of the night before, trying to imagine all of the possible reasons for a stranger to be standing outside the Mill in the pouring rain. But they came to no conclusions. The man in the green slicker raincoat was like a phantom who disappeared in the light of day.

They were determined to get something done at this lunch meeting that they had scheduled over a week ago, and at least try to put this mystery out of their minds for a bit. So they began discussing how to proceed with Moravian Days. The calendar for the event looked fine, especially since Adele booked the dates a good year in advance.

Moravian Days was the combined effort of the six local Moravian Churches, plus the Bethlehem Historical Society. A shared community ministry among the churches and other Moravian-related entities, Moravian Days was a popular time to gather and to open up the event to the community.

By holding the activities on Central's campus, folks would also have a chance to tour the historic buildings such as the 1741 Gemeinhaus, the 1751 Old Chapel and the 1806 Central Moravian Church sanctuary. Just down the hill, the buildings in the Moravian Industrial Quarter would also be open. People loved to see the 18 foot diameter water wheel turning in the 1762 Waterworks. They watched in amazement as the sparks flew when the blacksmiths worked hot iron over the anvil in the 1750 Smithy.

No one was more supportive of the event than the Rev. Dr. Baxter Hemphill, a colleague on Adele's staff as Visitation Pastor. He had planned to meet with the two women today, but was called out, once again, to deal with a family emergency.

"Baxter thinks that our ideas are great," Adele said as they looked over the menus. "I'm sure that he will do what he can to help promote Moravian Days."

Baxter was the kind of pastor who was a real cheerleader for his parishioners and the staff. He was the ultimate extrovert, who never missed an opportunity to talk about Central Church and to invite someone to come by on a Sunday morning to visit and worship.

It seemed like Baxter knew everyone in town, from retired executives to CEO's of new businesses in the area, to college presidents. His enthusiasm was contagious.

"As we get further along," Adele said, "let's get him involved in publicity, especially with the Moravian pastors. He is always good at rallying the troops."

"Absolutely," Mitzi said, glancing out of the window just as a familiar looking man in a green slicker raincoat walked by the Book Shop across the street.

"Look, that's the man!" she cried out, jumping up from her chair, almost knocking it over as she raced to the window.

"He is the guy I saw in the rain last night! He's wearing the same jacket and has the same build. I know that's the man."

As they stood at the tall arched window for a better look, a voice boomed out behind them, "Hello ladies! Something interesting out there?"

They turned around to see none other than their nemesis, Merrill Houser. Merrill was tall and rather gaunt looking, with thinning, brownish gray hair swept to one side of his forehead. The most remarkable thing about him were his glasses, large with heavy dark frames that gave him an owlish appearance.

The women sat down abruptly, not wanting to let him in on what they were looking at across Main Street. They purposely did not ask him to join them, hoping that Merrill would take the hint that they wanted some privacy. But quite a while later, Merrill was still standing there, talking away, as the waitress served them their dessert. He was rehashing his usual litany of concerns, everything from a dispute about where to plant a tree, to getting brighter lighting installed in the historic district. They'd heard it all before. Mercifully, his cell phone buzzed suddenly and he left to answer it.

"Do you believe that man? He is oblivious to anything but his own agenda."

"I think we lucked out. Doesn't look like he will be back," said Mitzi, glancing over toward the lobby as Merrill, still on his phone, was pushing open the heavy glass doors to leave.

"I didn't want to tell him this, but my volunteer Fred Lang has discovered some very interesting facts about a Jedediah Houser who lived in Bethlehem and served in the Civil War. I actually had someone else inquiring about the genealogy of a man who is connected to the Civil War in some way, a Mark Sargent. Fred is looking into his ancestors as well."

It was all very puzzling, and the details so far were sketchy. But why, after all these years, were Mark Sargent and Merrill Houser so eager to learn more about their family histories?

"We've got our own mystery to solve, Mitzi," said Adele. "The man in the rain is obviously still in town, if we just saw him. You should call the police and let them know."

"I could," said Mitzi, sipping her tea thoughtfully. "What could they really do though?" Looking at her watch she said with surprise, "Look how late it is! My next meeting is 20 minutes from now in Allentown. Could we get together again tomorrow around 4:30 in the Church office?"

"Perfect," said Adele, picking up the check over Mitzi's objections. "Since we didn't get too far today, I think I'll wait to see if Baxter can join us when we are further along in the planning."

CHAPTER FIVE

73 West Church Street

ADELE'S first meeting with the denominational review board, before she was accepted as a candidate for ministry, had taken place in the Church office Conference Room some 26 years ago.

How things changed and continued to change in the Church. When Adele came before the review board for approval as a candidate for ministry, not many women were serving as pastors anywhere in the country. These days, though, women were called to serve churches right out of seminary with very little question, especially in the north.

As she looked around her office, Adele remembered that Baxter Hemphill was the driving force behind Central Church's purchase of the office building. Or, to be more exact, it was Baxter who sought out and approached donors to help buy the building, before he retired. No one knew more about fundraising than Baxter. People liked Baxter and trusted him. His wife Ramona, a beautiful, accomplished woman who was very active in the community didn't hurt his popularity, either.

Like most pastors, Baxter put in crazy long hours, even though he was now semi-retired and part-time. Most Thursday mornings he came into the office to confer with staff, which included Margaret, the secretary and *de facto* office manager.

Without Margaret to keep the church calendar, there would have been terrible collisions among all of the entities that made use of historic Central Church day in and day out.

Margaret also handled the large volume of correspondence that Baxter was generating these days, as he worked on a special project among Bethlehem's retired clergy. As he usually did, he sat next to her desk in the outer office, reviewing messages. Being in the outer office meant that people were always coming and going, with phones ringing and staff checking in for mail and messages. That was all fine with Baxter, a people person if there ever was one.

That Thursday morning, Mark Sargent came into the office, glanced at the nicely decorated hallway with its antique furnishings and oil paintings and looked around the corner to see Baxter engrossed in the mail.

"Good morning," Baxter called out, seeing him standing there. He popped up from his chair and offered a vigorous handshake. "I'm Baxter Hemphill. What can I do for you?"

"Mark Sargent, Reverend. I am here to find some information about my family."

For the next 40 minutes or so, Baxter shared stories with Mark about the Moravians and how they aligned themselves during the Civil War and the Revolutionary War before that. He was a walking encyclopedia when it came to Moravians, and especially Bethlehem's Moravian history.

"Here is a book you'll want to read," said Baxter, handing Mark a copy of the book that he and Adele wrote a few years earlier, *Let Us Go Over to Bethlehem - A Guide To The Moravian Community.*

As Mark paged through the book, Baxter pointed out some of the features of the office building itself. The conference room was home to the Ladies' Sewing Society, a group that had been in existence and active since the days of the Civil War, when its members knitted stockings for the troops. Now the dozen or so ladies who gathered every week made the Polly Heckewelder dolls, selling them to raise funds for the causes they supported.

The ladies were known for keeping good records, so Baxter advised Mark to contact the Sewing Society. Their records just might note something about Private Joe Carver as a recipient of a pair or two of the warm stockings that their great-great-great grandmothers knitted for the soldiers.

Almost late for his next appointment, Baxter skillfully steered Mark toward the door, said goodbye and got ready to leave.

As he glanced out the window he saw Adele pulling into the parking lot. "Hey, how are you?" he called as she came up the back stairs. As he dropped off a document for Margaret to mail and started to leave through the front door he said, "Let's get together sometime this week."

"I'll check my calendar and let you know," Adele said.

Later that afternoon, Mitzi and Adele spread out their notes and calendars on the conference table, tying together some loose ends and finalizing the budget for their Moravian Days event.

As they finished and cleared off the conference table for the staff meeting the next morning, Mitzi asked, "Have you told Baxter about the stranger in the rain?"

"Not yet," Adele replied, turning out the tall brass floor lamps surrounding the conference table, gifts from the Sewing Society, of course. "I may give him a call this evening."

"Here is another piece of our Merrill Houser mystery. Fred told me this afternoon that Mark's Sargent's great-great-great grandfather and Merrill's may have known each other back in the time of the Civil War. Apparently, the two men were waiting to leave Bethlehem for active duty back in October of 1862, when there was a shooting. Fred will be speaking with Elaine Ettwein, who has done extensive research about her family tree and relatives who served during the war. He's going to meet with her tomorrow."

It wasn't until after the next morning's staff meeting that Adele could talk with Baxter about their experience at the Mill. He nodded thought-fully, but didn't say much. Adele wondered if he thought that they were being overly dramatic about what happened.

Changing the subject, he leaned back in his chair and said, "Yesterday a young man stopped in the office asking a lot of questions about the Moravians' involvement in the Civil War. We talked for a while and you know me, Adele, I loaded him down with information, including our book. He said that his great-great-great grandfather was a Union soldier who may have been murdered here in town. That's the first time I heard that story."

"Mitzi's volunteer, Fred Lang is hoping to find out more about that relative. He is digging into Merrill Houser's family tree and…"

"Merrill Houser? Why would she want to get involved with Houser?" Baxter was not especially a fan of Mr. Houser, starting a few years ago when Houser challenged him at a meeting. It was very clear that the intent of Houser's remarks was to embarrass the church.

"I think that Mitzi wanted to put an end to Merrill's badgering her about his family history. And that Mark Sargent was asking about his family.

"At any rate, Mark Sargent's name came up in the materials that Fred found. I wonder, could it be that his great-great-great grandfather may have been done in by Houser's?"

"My, my," said Baxter with a smile. "I knew Houser had some skeletons in his closet, I just didn't know that they were of the historical type."

"Baxter, we need to look in the church diary. Who was the Pastor in the 1860's? Did he write anything about the Houser family or Joe Carver?"

"Adele, call the Archivist. All of our old diaries are at the Moravian Archives."

There was a short tap on the conference room door as Margaret interrupted to tell Baxter that his wife was on the phone.

"Let's keep talking about this story. Sounds like grist for another book," Baxter teased. Actually, that's not a bad idea, Adele pondered. "Murder Among the Moravians." Who would have thought?

CHAPTER SIX

Family Trees

ELAINE Ettwein was proud of her husband's family and its deep roots within the Bethlehem community.

Over the years, Elaine had come to love researching the Ettwein genealogy. After her husband passed away, her reading and research made her feel that she was still close to him. So when Fred Lang called her that morning, she was pleased to share some of her findings with him, not only about the Ettweins, but about other Bethlehem families whose ancestors had become like old friends.

Fred knew a bit about the Merrill Houser family tree, but Elaine doubted that he knew much about the connection between Jedediah Houser and Joe Carver, husband of Mary Ettwein Carver.

Later that afternoon, Fred appeared on her doorstep, just as Elaine was saying goodbye to her daughter, Beth.

"Not joining us today?" asked Fred.

Beth laughed, "You know that you are in good hands with my mother, Mr. Lang. She's the family expert! Nice to see you again."

"Nice to see you, too," Fred replied.

Elaine showed Fred to her sunny dining room, where books and papers were spread across the table, ready for Elaine to share what she'd learned.

"Fred, you may know already, I believe, that John Ettwein, who lived in the late 1770's, had been adopted into the Ettwein family. His grand-daughter, Mary Ettwein married Joe Carver, from the Swiftwater area in the Poconos. Unfortunately, Mary died in childbirth, and her husband Joe was killed in Bethlehem just before he was set to leave with his regiment at the start of the Civil War.

"Perhaps Mary and Joe's child was told, or perhaps he wasn't, that his father was killed. At any rate, Ettwein family journals speculate about the story of Joe's death at the hands of Jedediah Houser. There is a note in one journal that says that Mary Carver was supposed to travel to Bethlehem to retrieve a gift that Joe left for her. But of course, she would not have been able to travel because she was pregnant. And then, sadly, she died in giving birth.

"I think that in order to understand more completely about both the Houser family and the Carver family, we need to do a bit more digging. There may be a lot more to learn about how and why Joe was killed."

"Agreed," said Fred, already making notes about Elaine's story and about where they could go to explore to find out more. The Bethlehem Public Library was a place to visit, and certainly the Moravian Archives.

"Maybe we could take a field trip or two," said Elaine. "We might find a newspaper story or church record from 1862 that might shed some light on what actually happened between Joe and Jedediah."

"Great idea. Just let me know when we can meet."

Soon after Fred left, Elaine was able to set up a time to meet at the Moravian Archives. Elaine could almost guess what they would find: a sad story about a young soldier who was killed by a fellow soldier and whose final gift to his wife and child was hidden somewhere in Bethlehem. She ached for the families of those times, whose sons and daughters faced danger at every turn and died far too soon.

Life is always too fragile, she thought as she looked around at the books and paintings and all of the cherished mementoes of her husband and the life they shared together for so many years.

But life doesn't stop, she told herself resolutely, clearing off the table for dinner. The future always holds the promise of happiness ahead.

Town was busy that afternoon. The lovely spring weather continued to bring people out onto Main Street. A man in a dark green slicker blended into the crowds as he walked up the sheltered entryway to the Moravian Book Shop.

Mitzi's in-laws, Vaughn's parents, Brett and Cecilia, loved shopping on Main Street. Whenever they came to town, they enjoyed walking around the historic district, visiting the museums and historic sites, stopping at one of the restaurants for lunch. Today, they were on their way home to Connecticut from a trip to Florida. They decided to stay overnight in Bethlehem. As usual, they made their way to the Book Shop before going to meet Mitzi and Vaughn for dinner.

Browsing through the book department, an older section of the shop, with its creaky wooden floors and sharp angled, packed displays of books, they literally bumped into the stranger in the green slicker. He was poring over a book from the Moravian shelf and seemed oblivious to Brett.

"Excuse me," said Brett with a friendly smile. "Sorry! Kind of tight quarters in here. Are you reading up on your Moravian history?"

"Yes, I am looking for information about the Colonial Industrial Quarter, especially the Tannery," said the stranger, quickly replacing the book on the shelf.

"Well, this is a good place to start," said Brett. "Our daughter-in-law may be able to help you, too. She is head of the local historical society. Just go up the street to the Visitor Center and one of her staff can give you lots of information about the historic industrial area."

"Thanks, I'll keep that in mind," said the stranger as he backed away and headed for the side door.

Later that evening at dinner, they recounted their stop in South Carolina on their way north to visit Cecilia's cousins. After opening the gifts that they brought, Mitzi asked, "So was it crowded in town today?"

"Definitely," said Cecilia.

"Really crowded," said Brett, "In fact, I almost knocked over a man in the book department. He seemed a little odd to me, kind of secretive. But he said he wanted to know more about the Industrial Quarter. So I gave him your name and sent him to your Visitor Center. I didn't get his name, though."

"He was a little odd," chimed in Cecilia. "Plus it was rather warm for the green slicker he was wearing."

Mitzi nearly dropped her fork, startled. "What? Did you say he was wearing a green slicker?"

Mitzi got up and immediately called her Visitor Center manager.

"Kim, sorry to bother you this evening, but did you happen to see a man in a green slicker come into the Visitor Center this afternoon?"

"As a matter of fact, yes. He was very strange, wearing a slicker on such a lovely spring day. He wanted information about the Tannery. So we asked him if he wanted to take a tour of the area, but when we tried to get his name and contact information, he turned pretty abruptly and left the shop."

"Thanks, Kim. I'll explain tomorrow."

Cecilia and Brett looked concerned as Mitzi and Vaughn shared the story of the rainy night and that stranger in the green slicker.

CHAPTER SEVEN

Visitor at the Moravian Archives

THE Moravian Archives was housed in a contemporary, one story brick building on Locust Street in Bethlehem.

Inside the Archives, past the spacious reading room, were two massive temperature-controlled vaults. In them were stored many of the documents and treasures of Moravian Bethlehem's past.

Visitors to the Archives were always welcome, although Archivist Dr. Peter Johansen preferred to have people call in advance before they came in. The staff was limited to himself, his assistant Eric Kelly and a secretary, Louise. Patrice Guillaume also had an office in the building, as Assistant Director of the Moravian Music Foundation.

A bell toned quietly as the front door of the Archives opened and a man walked into the reception area and approached Louise's desk. Just then, Peter stepped in from the reading room and greeted the man.

"Norman Sterner," the man said, tentatively, as Peter reached out to shake his hand. "I need to look up some information about the Colonial Industrial Quarter at the time of the Civil War."

"I would be glad to introduce you to our colleague, Eric. He will help you locate what you need. Come in and have a seat."

"I'm going to need it as soon as possible," said Sterner.

Fortunately, the Archives had just hired Eric, who could help with the walk-in visitors. However, Sterner's abrupt attitude and the fact that he hadn't called ahead made Peter reluctant to offer the man unlimited time with Eric.

Urgency was a strange sort of thing at the Archives. After all, the history of Moravians in Bethlehem was well documented and had always been preserved carefully and patiently. "Emergency" historical research seemed an oxymoron, thought Peter, unless there were a special circumstance.

After introducing Sterner to Eric, Peter went back to his office. There were a number of calls to return, and he had hoped to complete an article for a professional journal before the end of the day. Mercifully, the phones stayed quiet.

Eric listened to Mr. Sterner's requests, and brought some documents out of the vault for him to review. Peter called to Eric to come into the office to assist with a telephone call from a pastor in Ohio looking for information.

After their phone conference call ended, Eric went back to the reading room and saw that it was empty.

He immediately called to Peter, "What happened to Mr. Sterner? I didn't see him leave."

Peter walked quickly from his office to the reading room.

Just then, the thick, metal door to the south vault opened and Sterner hustled out, carrying a bundle of what looked like architectural drawings.

"Did you need more help?" asked Peter. He was concerned that Sterner was actually trying to take the documents out of the building. Interestingly, he could see that they were old maps of Bethlehem.

"Eric can bring you anything else you need. Normally we ask that visitors not enter the vaults and definitely not remove items from the stacks themselves."

"I was just returning them," Sterner said quickly.

"No need. I will take them," Peter said, reaching out for the papers.

"I'll see myself out," mumbled Sterner.

Peter looked at the man as he hurriedly left the building, zipping up his dark green slicker. As the man made his way down the flagstone steps to the street, Peter made a mental note to have Eric check the vault.

When Peter got back to his office, the phone rang. "Hi Peter. I'm calling with another one of my famous questions."

It was not unusual for Adele to pick up the phone and call Peter for quick answers to questions about the old Moravian Congregation of Bethlehem, or historical details about the Christmas traditions such as the Putz, a Nativity display that was erected every year in the Christian

Education Building. In fact, she jokingly referred to her ongoing conversations with him as "archivist abuse." But he never seemed to mind.

From time to time, after a Church History Committee meeting, Peter and Adele talked about some of the mysteries of the Church's collection of artifacts. But today, it was not about the artifacts, rather it was about a stranger in a green slicker.

"Adele, you will not believe what happened a few minutes ago,"

CHAPTER EIGHT

The Archivist's Story

ADELE was intrigued when Peter told her the story of the visit of Norman Sterner. "So what did you think of him? What is he after, do you suppose?"

"Well, I doubt that he was doing research on family history. I caught him coming out of the vault with a stack of maps and drawings under his arm that didn't have anything to do with family history. He looked very uncomfortable that I caught him. He should not have been in the vault alone."

After hearing that Peter had concerns, Adele told him about the man in the green slicker, standing out in the rain the other night. If he were the same man, it was certainly time to start connecting the dots, and time to be suspicious of Sterner's real motives.

Adele also asked him about the Church diary from the 1860s. Peter told her he would research that time period.

With a promise to keep each other updated, Peter and Adele said goodbye, neither knowing what the next step should be. But in Norman Sterner, she knew that they had found another mystery to pursue. She immediately called Mitzi.

"We finally have a name for the man in the green slicker. Norman Sterner!"

"And you won't believe *this*, but Vaughn's parents literally bumped into him in one of the aisles of the Book Shop!"

Adele hung up the phone and sat back in her desk chair. She went over the situation in her mind, wondering who in the world this man was and why he was in town.

It was after 5 pm now and the rest of the staff left at 4:30. The office was quiet.

She was so caught up in her thoughts that she was startled when she heard Baxter's voice booming from the first floor.

"You still here? Stay there, I'll come to you. Can't stay long," he said, "Ramona has us serving dinner at the shelter this evening. I won't keep you but a minute. Got a call today from Beth Ettwein."

"Beth! I haven't heard from her in a while. She is such a sweetheart. Is she in town?"

Beth had been a part of the small group of young adults that was active when Adele first came to the Church. Beth remained a member even after she moved out to the Midwest for grad school. But whenever she was in town, they made it a point to get together.

"Yes, she is home visiting her mother. She actually just called earlier and wanted to speak with you, but I saw that you were on the phone."

"I was speaking with Peter. You wouldn't believe what he told me about the man he encountered today at the Archives."

"I'll bet he gets all kinds of characters dropping in," Baxter said, bouncing up from his chair, not picking up on the story.

"While I have you here," Adele said, paging through her calendar, "Are you available to meet with Mitzi and me about Moravian Days? Are you in the office tomorrow?"

"All day," said Baxter. "Just let me know when you and Mitzi are available."

"Sure, sounds good. Have a good time at the shelter."

CHAPTER NINE

Living History

MEETING with Baxter and Adele was important, even though Mitzi was incredibly busy this whole month. If they could make some final decisions and set the wheels in motion, they would not have to reconvene again until well into next year.

Mitzi preferred planning for things in advance, although she was not opposed to spontaneity. Sometimes the best events happened on the spur of the moment. By using social media and email blasts to her member and friend lists, her office was able to get the word out about guest speakers who happened to be in town for the day, or an impromptu luncheon prior to a press conference announcing a new exhibit at one of the Society's museums.

As she thought about it, she realized that an item on the Moravian Days agenda should be publicity. Not only was print publicity important, but email and social media were all realities to be embraced in this new age of technology, even for an historical society.

Making some mental notes to talk with Baxter and Adele, she gathered her tablet and some lists from their previous meeting, stuck them in a leather folder and left from the back door of the Kemerer Museum. It was a brief, two block walk along Church Street to the Church office. Just taking this short walk was like walking back through time. She often daydreamed about what it might have been like to live in this amazing community hundreds of years ago. Mitzi always felt inspired by the architecture of these 1700's Colonial Germanic-style stone buildings with their brick arches over the windows and herringbone-patterned doors. Some of these 18th century structures were still being used for their original purposes.

She crossed Church Street to the office building, went up the flagstone front steps and opened the door. A voice boomed from the back of the sunny hallway, "Here she is," said Baxter, who was standing at the back door talking with a visitor.

"Mitzi, please meet Mark Sargent. He is in town doing some research on his family's history. Mark, Mitzi here is a wonderful person for you to get to know."

"So nice to match a face with a name," Mitzi said, extending her hand. "Since our phone conversation several weeks ago, I've had a researcher gathering information about your family. We'll have to get together while you are in town."

Just then, Adele popped her head from the workroom doorway. "Hi there," she said, "I'll be with you all in a moment. Nice to meet you, Mark."

Mark nodded and shook hands with Baxter and thanked him for his time. "I'm looking forward to meeting with you, Mitzi. I'll call your office to make an appointment," he said as he was leaving.

"Come on back," said Baxter to Mitzi. "I hear that we are going to spend some time together today to wrap things up for our program next year."

"That sounds like a tall order," laughed Mitzi, as she walked into the conference room with him and sat down at the large, polished oak conference table that was used for church board meetings.

As the three of them talked, it became clear that all three were looking forward to Moravian Days as a way for the Church and Society to present themselves to the community.

"You're doing a great job at the Society," said Baxter sincerely. "You are a person who makes things happen."

"More like a labor of love," Mitzi laughed. "I have had some great advice from people like you and from our friend, Radcliffe Rhoad."

Radcliffe was the retired historian who advised groups like the Society on architectural issues. He and Vaughn and Mitzi had become fast friends through their contacts involving the Historic Landmark District.

"I'm just sorry that you had to deal with the scare at the Mill a few days ago," said Adele.

"I dragged you into that, didn't I? Did you tell Baxter that Vaughn's parents actually bumped into our mystery man at the Book Shop?"

"Yes, she told me," said Baxter. "I heard that Peter met him too, and thought that he was a little strange."

"At least we finally know his name."

Margaret tapped on the door before she stepped into the room with a phone message slip for Baxter. "I thought you were almost finished, so I told him that you'd call him back soon. Sounded urgent."

Baxter said his goodbyes and Adele walked Mitzi to the door. "I might stop by the Kemerer to see you next week. Beth Ettwein's in town and I'd like her to see the renovations you've done."

"Good idea! I'd love to see Beth again," said Mitzi. "She is such a wonderful person. Her mom has been a loyal friend of the Society ever since it began. It was sad that her dad passed away last year. He was a great board member; he was so convinced that we have an important story to tell here in Bethlehem. That family has a long history dating back to the 1700's. As you well know, Adele, we even have an Ettwein Street!"

"Beth's father was a good friend to Zeke and me when I first started at Central. Beth comes from a great family, doesn't she? I'll give you a call before we come by, probably early next week."

As she went upstairs to her office, Adele remembered that she had heard that Beth was 'single' again. Beth had written to Adele that she had broken up with her long-time boyfriend in Chicago around Thanksgiving. The matchmaking gene must have been a part of Adele's make up, she had to admit, because now she felt that she had a mission. Were there any eligible bachelors who would be good for Beth to meet? Wouldn't it be nice for Beth to settle down, maybe even here in town? She would have to give it some thought.

CHAPTER TEN

An Unwelcome Visitor

T HE weekend after the storm was a hectic one in Bethlehem. A sidewalk arts and crafts show drew thousands of people to Main Street. The merchants were in their glory. The stores were packed that Saturday afternoon. The restaurant owners downtown were happy to accommodate diners who crowded around their outdoor tables.

Sunday worship services at Central Moravian Church drew lots of visitors at this time of year. Some were in town for graduations at Moravian College or Lehigh University. Visitors staying at Hotel Bethlehem, just across the street walked over to the Church sanctuary, drawn by the organ music that they heard reverberating through the 200 year old building. Some timidly stepped inside and were greeted by sacristans, who welcomed them with a handshake and a bulletin for the service.

Adele wondered who might be in the congregation on any given Sunday. Visitors of note had included writers, musicians, politicians, and even the stray actor now and then. The challenge for the pastors who were conducting the service was not to react too obviously when they spotted a VIP in the pews.

While visiting dignitaries were always a possibility, visitors who had more ulterior motives could be in the pews as well, she supposed. Every now and then, Adele would ponder what she would do if someone in the congregation stood up on a Sunday morning and threatened people with a weapon. It wasn't some farfetched scenario. These terrible things seemed to be happening more and more in churches and schools and movie theaters. It was in the news all the time.

During her many years at the church, though, the closest thing to a violent incident occurred when Jan Chapman, a feisty red haired lady in her 70's collapsed in the aisle during the beginning of the service. Word came back from a sacristan who accompanied Jan to the hospital with the paramedics that Jan was fine, but that she was really, really angry that she missed the Advent liturgy.

Back in 1999, the turn of the calendar had made Adele jumpy about what might happen that New Year's Eve. She was scheduled to preach at the 11:30 pm Vigil Service. Crazy people might be using this once in a lifetime turn of the millennium event to start acting out.

"What happens if someone stands up and starts threatening me when I'm speaking?" she asked Zeke. "Duck," he answered with a grin.

Adele recalled hitting him with a pillow for that remark. But nothing happened at the service, except for a few extra fireworks going off at the stroke of midnight. Actually, the Bethlehem Area Moravians' Trombone Choir traditionally interrupted the pastor during the sermon, at the stroke of midnight, as a surprise, and in line with the biblical warning that one never knew the hour when the Lord would return. In practice, however, the trombonists would start to play a minute or two before midnight, to beat the fireworks that rattled the huge windows of the sanctuary.

What about today, on this beautiful bright Sunday morning? Who would be in Church today? Certainly not someone wanting to do harm.

In the back row of the sanctuary, closest to the Main Street door, sat Norman Sterner, ignoring the music, the sermon and the hymns, with that green slicker thrown over the back of the pew. He was waiting for the service to end so that he could follow someone into the Church office building across the street. Perhaps church records could give him the answers he needed.

Adele was the first to get to the Church office across the street after the 11 am worship service. That was very unusual for her. Handshaking at the door and talking with parishioners were a big part of the pastoral contact that she looked forward to each Sunday. Baxter felt the same way as she. This morning, she said a quick goodbye to Baxter and gathered her purse and keys and ran across Church Street, missing even the first of the cars pulling out of the lot.

She'd scheduled a pre-marital counseling session for 12:15 pm and just made it to the office in time to find the young couple already on the doorstep.

Adele greeted them, unlocked the door and showed them into the Pearl Frantz Parlor, just off the hall to the right. She closed the hall door, the top of which was glass and carefully curtained in beige voile on the street side to give the entryway a finished look.

As she glanced at her own reflection in the glass, suddenly a man stepped behind her.

Startled, she turned and all that she could take in was the dark green slicker.

"Oh, I didn't know that anyone was here," she said hurriedly, looking over to the couple snuggled together on the white brocade settee. "I have a counseling session."

"I must see some Church records as soon as possible," he said.

"Well, I'm sorry, but you will just have to come back tomorrow, Mr. …?"

"Sterner," he said abruptly, unconcerned with the couple in the parlor. "I'll be here tomorrow morning."

As he left, she closed the door behind him, wondering how he'd managed to get in the office. Was it a sacristan who let him in? Or perhaps it was someone who left an adult class meeting in the building earlier and forgot to lock up.

At any rate, she found herself still shaking a bit as she took a seat in the blue brocade wing chair across from the young couple. Norman Sterner, the man in the green slicker, was now very real to her.

As she talked with the young couple about their wedding plans, her mind kept wandering back to the rainy night at the Mill.

CHAPTER ELEVEN

Clues to the Mystery

ONDAYS were supposed to be "catch up" days for the Historical Society. Its museums were closed, but business went on as usual in their offices. Last week's flooding and storm damage had been minor, fortunately, with the exception of the broken window on the third floor of the Mill.

Two weeks ago, Mark Sargent had contacted Mitzi, saying that he was coming to Bethlehem soon and hoping to find information about his ancestors. He made an appointment to see her today and now sat across from her at the wide antique desk, stacked with correspondence and files. He carefully opened a small manila envelope and handed her the original pen and ink letter from his ancestor, Joe Carver, to his wife, Mary Ettwein Carver, written so long ago.

Slowly and carefully unfolding the delicate piece of paper, laying it flat on her desk, Mitzi realized that she was touching a piece of Civil War history. She was also mindful of the importance of this letter to Mark.

With a sense of both excitement and reverence, she began to read quietly,

11th of October, 1862

My Dearest Mary,

You have given me your locket to carry with me into war, but I fear for its safety. I will always hold you dear to my heart and never forget your sweetness.

I will find a safe hiding place here at the old Tannery to place your locket and I am also leaving my pocket watch for you. We have been playing cards, waiting for our time to go, and I have done well. I will leave something else here for you and our baby, so that if anything should happen to me, you will be provided for. Please make haste. I do not trust sending these to you.

I will ask the pastor of the Church on the hill to post this letter for me. Go and speak with him. He will direct you to the Tannery. I have no time to return to our farm. We leave on the morrow.

Your loving husband,

Joe

"What a touching letter," Mitzi said, handing it back to Mark. "But it also has a sense of urgency about it, too, doesn't it?"

"Joe was afraid that someone was stalking him, apparently," said Mark, carefully slipping the letter back into the file he had brought with him.

"Mark, our genealogy researcher, Fred, has come up with some references to Joe Carver, your great-great-great grandfather. But one story isn't something that we can authenticate.

"One of our old-timers here in Bethlehem with a lot of local stories is Nellie Titherington. She says that she remembers her grandfather telling her about the body of a young soldier that was found in the Tannery vat. Nellie's grandfather was just a young boy at the time, too young to go to war, helping with some construction work in the Industrial Quarter. The workers were rebuilding the vat space the day after the soldiers left town and they found the body. She said that the young soldier's name was Joe Carver."

Mitzi looked closely at Mark's face to see his reaction to this grim piece of information. To her, Mark looked like an athlete, tanned, nice looking, in his early 30's perhaps. He looked more like he would be at home on a football field than sitting in a chair in her office. His face was stoic. She went on...

"Fred just started looking for references to Joe's death in the newspaper records of the time. There was suspicion that Joe was murdered for his money. The soldiers were gambling at the rooming house across Water Street from the Tannery, before they were to be shipped out.

"Joe missed the train and no one knew what happened to him until days later.

"It was such a chaotic time with people going off to war. Fred still has more research to do. But this letter suggests that Joe certainly had something he wanted to protect for his young wife and future child."

Mark nodded slowly, sitting back in the chair. "I wondered," he said. "Our family stories always included the hint that Joe's death was not actually in combat, nor was it accidental."

He went on to explain that his mother, Shirley Carver Sargent, had been the real keeper of the Carver family history. She carefully preserved the few written records of Joe Carver and some of the letters that he had written to his young wife, Mary.

Mark always knew that his mother had an interest in family history, but it wasn't until after his mother's death from cancer earlier this year that he had found evidence that she had a real passion for learning more about the tragic Carver family legacy.

Mitzi was curious about how the family papers got passed down from generation to generation.

Mark explained, "When Mary died, Joe's parents put all of Mary and Joe's personal belongings in a trunk for safe keeping for this precious baby boy, so that when he grew up, he would have something of his parents. After a while, the trunk was forgotten in a corner of their farmhouse attic in Swiftwater. It wasn't until my mother started trying to find out about her ancestors that the trunk was discovered."

"It would be very difficult to find out exactly what happened to Joe Carver," Mitzi said. "But we can make a guess...

"We do know that Joe was in Bethlehem, probably awaiting deployment with his unit. Most of the troops stayed in boarding houses around town until their units were ready to leave. There were rooms on the upper floors inside the Tannery itself during those years.

"Perhaps, during the wait, Joe got into a card game and when he found himself losing, he put up his wife's locket as part of the stakes and then lost everything. Maybe he was able somehow to take it back in secret and that's why he wrote to Mary that he was hiding it for safekeeping."

"But according to the letter Joe won at cards and his killer wanted his money back. So he killed Joe either by accident or intentionally."

"But before he was killed, apparently Joe was able to hide the locket and the money and give the letter to the pastor whom he trusted, to mail."

"Maybe none of this is relevant at all," said Mark. "But I would like to do some more investigating, as a way of honoring my mother, if for no other reason. She was a very sweet person. Too nice, maybe for her own good."

"What do you mean?"

"I probably shouldn't tell you this," said Mark, "but it may add some pieces to the puzzle if you knew that she became friends with an antiques dealer in Swiftwater, a Warren Pritchard. He didn't have a very good reputation in the Pocono area. He always undervalued the items that people brought to him, wanting to buy them for a lot less than they were worth. He was more about money than history.

"He got to know my mother through a friend of hers who told him Joe Carver's story. I would have to say that it was after that time that he became very attentive to my mother. I think that she started to depend on him more and more. Too much, I think. She may have even thought that he had a romantic interest in her. She'd been a widow for over seven years at that point, and I know that she was very lonely after my dad died.

"At any rate, she showed Joe's letter to Warren, along with some objects that had been passed down through the family.

"When she died, he was the first person to come to me to ask if he could buy her collection of letters and memorabilia. He was very cold about it, very calculating, like it was just a business deal to him. He didn't care for my mother at all.

"It wasn't right," continued Mark, tears beginning to form in his eyes. "She trusted him and cared for him. It was obvious that all he wanted was the collection."

"I am so sorry for your loss," Mitzi said softly. "You didn't deserve to have to deal with this person so soon after your mother passed away."

"Now you can see why I want to know as much as I can about our family. It isn't really about the history, it's about my mother." Forcing a smile, he stood up and extended his hand to Mitzi. "Thanks so much for talking with me."

"I'll be in touch if there is anything else we can find. Are you staying at the Hotel?"

"Yes, I'm here for the next few days, at least." With his file folder under his arm, he walked out of her office and down the hall. Mitzi watched him from her window as he walked slowly past the Tannery, stopping for a moment and then walking up the hill toward the Hotel.

How incredible it is that history intersects with who we are today, she thought. A family's history is precious because it helps to shape the identity of that family. To the Carver family, the value of that history itself was so emotionally charged. Joe Carver was a soldier who showed the courage of a soldier, willing to fight for a cause. But Joe was also a loving husband to Mary, and the fierce loyalty and love he felt for her also defined who he was. As it happened, according to what Mark had uncovered, Joe was also the father of a child whom he would never get to see. Mary was pregnant with his child before Joe left Swiftwater. She died in childbirth. That very child's great-great-great grandson had just left Mitzi's office.

Joe and Mary Carver's poignant story would have been just that; a tragic set of circumstances that left another child orphaned by war. Some nagging questions remained: Who killed Joe and why was an antiques dealer in the Poconos so eager to locate his meager belongings of a locket, a pocket watch and possibly some coins?

With the museums closed, Mitzi thought that Monday mornings were to be the quiet time for catching up. Today was anything but!

.

CHAPTER TWELVE

Matchmakers

IF there were any other young woman from Bethlehem who was as active in the community and as genuinely nice a person as Beth Ettwein, Adele didn't know who it could be.

Beth graduated with honors from Liberty High School and Moravian College, majoring in music. From her earliest days at Moravian, Beth became the creative energy behind the College's partnership with the young people of the city in music education and community concerts. She was also a Junior Guide at one of the Society's museums. A petite, blond-haired dynamo, Beth was one of those people who always made Adele smile.

Since Mitzi hadn't seen Beth in a long time, Adele invited her to join them for lunch. It would be a great time, as always, because Beth was one of those rare people who could be comfortable with people of any age. Beth was only in her late 20's and Adele and Mitzi were two mature women; their ages never seemed to be a barrier to their friendship.

Adele looked out a window in the Church office, just as Beth pulled into the lot, got out of her car, then spied Adele at the window, waved and started towards the back steps.

Just at that moment, Baxter bounded around the building toward the parking lot with Mark Sargent in tow. Of course, there were introductions all around, Baxter believing that everyone should know everyone else in town.

Mark nodded at Beth as she smiled and said, "I guess you figured it out that Rev. Hemphill knows everyone in Bethlehem."

They all laughed, and from what Adele could see from her window of this little exchange, there were definitely some sparks flying between

Beth and Mark. As she came in the back door, Beth even whispered to Adele, "He's cute!"

The restaurant they chose, the Café, was in a big old home on the west side of Bethlehem. Its wide front porch was spacious enough for tables and chairs for dining outside. Inside, the individual rooms were kept intact, like a home, with tables set in the midst of charming old furniture, silk flowers and ferns. They were seated by the owner on the first floor near the large, ornate marble fireplace. The restaurant was beginning to fill up, but it felt more intimate than cramped. Conversations at the tables were lively and filled with laughter.

As they were looking over their menus, Adele started teasing Beth about Mark and that accidental encounters could lead to something interesting.

"We know that you're always the matchmaker, Adele," Mitzi scolded her with a hint of a smile, "But in this case, you may be on to something."

"Cut it out, you two," said Beth. "Maybe I'll bump into him again, maybe not. For now, let's just order our lunch."

Over their salads, Mitzi told Adele and Beth about Mark's mission to find out more about Joe Carver. They listened intently and felt a pang of sadness for Mark as he tried to do what he could to honor his mother's memory.

"He's staying at the Hotel," Mitzi said, concluding her story.

"So am I," laughed Beth. "My mom's doing some renovations at our house, so there is no room for me at the inn!" Beth's mother, Elaine, was an interior designer whose home was a showcase already. Beth was puzzled about why her mother was clearing out a spare bedroom to use as a study, but that was Elaine, always changing things around and making the old home even more gorgeous.

"You poor thing," said Adele in mock pain, "Now you'll be forced to see Mark at breakfast tomorrow morning!"

No one can really predict how these things happen. Romance is something you can't force, and it just doesn't materialize over a steamy, lingering glance, like in the movies. But something did happen between Mark and Beth at their first chance encounter, something that led to them running into each other, accidentally, of course, at breakfast in the hotel dining room; something that led to them bumping into each other in the hotel parking deck later that morning.

Without any of Adele's matchmaking assistance, they found themselves becoming friends. As Mark shared the story of his search for family secrets with her, Beth became his partner in crime. Together, they hiked around the Industrial Quarter, toured the buildings that were open to the public, stopping at the Smithy and walking through the Goundie House exhibit. But the best times were their early evening walks through the Central Church Green under the tall old trees, and their stops to rest on the massive, curved brownstone steps of the Church overlooking Main Street.

Together they imagined what it might have been like for the flood of men to have poured into town to be mustered into the army. What was young Joe Carver thinking as he walked these grounds before his unit was to leave for battle? He must have missed his young wife back home in Swiftwater, not knowing when he would see her again, if ever.

As Mark and Beth talked about love and loyalty and devotion to country, they grew closer and more determined to try to find out what really happened to Joe.

Beth and Mark decided to join forces with Elaine and Fred to scour all the records of the time. They also decided to meet with Merrill, much to their dismay. Since his family story was closely tied to the Ettwein and Carver family histories, too, maybe something helpful would come to light.

Two of them went to the Archives to check the Church records and the other two went to the public library to look for newspaper articles. They met up later at the Society's Archives to share their findings and to see what new details might have been uncovered.

Meanwhile, Mitzi and Adele went to visit Nellie Titherington again. Nellie told them that her elders were always speculating that Jedediah was never right after the war. He turned to drink, and died in a flood shortly after he came back from the war. He often mumbled that he was sorry for what he did. No one ever thought that he actually killed Joe Carver.

CHAPTER THIRTEEN

Two Sleuths at Gunpoint

MITZI decided to follow through on her own investigation of Mark's great-great-great grandfather, Joe Carver. So late on that Friday afternoon, she called Adele to join her at the Tannery to hear about the most recent discussion she had with Radcliffe Rhoad, the historian and preservationist whose opinion she valued so much.

Adele was happy to join her at the Tannery. Zeke, as usual was playing basketball with a group of guys on Sand Island. Her husband never missed a chance to play, not noticing, or not minding anyway, the bumps and bruises he got in fair exchange for a good workout.

As Mitzi left her office to walk across the grounds to the Tannery, she felt a tinge of uneasiness. The Tannery was an architecturally beautiful industrial building constructed in 1761. But even so, she always felt a sense of foreboding when she entered this massive stone structure. It was just a feeling she had, a bone-chilling coldness at any time of year.

She kept telling herself that she was not superstitious. But there were times, even in the Old Mill, that she was sure that someone was walking around on the upper floor, when she knew for certain that she was in the building alone.

Well, Mitzi thought, my staff is right across the grounds and I am making *myself* scared. This is ridiculous. She opened the heavy door and went inside.

"Are you there?" Adele called out a few minutes later as she opened one of the heavy, wooden, herringbone-patterned doors to the Tannery. It was a bit dark inside the large old stone building, after coming in from the brilliant late afternoon sunshine outside.

"Right here," Mitzi answered. "Come over here. I want to show you something."

Her eyes adjusting to the dark room, Adele walked across the room to where Mitzi stood, holding a small tin box.

"What is it?"

"This may have been what Mark was looking for. This box was hidden behind one of the loose stones near the stairs over the tanning vats."

"How on earth did you find it?"

"Remember I said that Radcliffe knew all about these old buildings? He gave me a clue about where to look for something that someone might tuck away, like a small object, so that it could be completely hidden. He told me that where wooden steps were cut into the stone walls, space might sometimes be left and loose stones placed to fill in. That could be where someone might be able to hide something."

"I decided to look for loose stones, and just by luck, I pushed a stone right here, and it moved! So I dug it out, ruining my nails, I might add! And this is what I found!"

Mitzi opened the tin box and inside was a small brown canvas pouch containing a pocket watch and a gold locket and chain. Carefully prying open the locket, they saw a small photo of a young woman on one side of the hinged locket and a photo of a young man on the other.

"This is it!" exclaimed Adele. "You found it! Was the money there, too, that the letter mentioned?"

"Yes, let's see. Just four or five of these coins," she said, emptying out the pouch. "Less than I thought, but still…"

Just then, across from them, the door creaked open and sunlight slanted across the dark floor.

Mitzi quickly slipped the locket, watch, and coins back into the pouch, put it into the tin box and closed the lid. With Adele standing directly in front of her, Mitzi was able to slide the box back into its hiding place in the wall.

"Who is it?" Adele called out to the figure whose face was half-hidden in the shadow of the doorway. As soon as he spoke, Adele knew it was the man she encountered that Sunday in the Church office.

"I know you found something. It's my property now and I mean to take it with me," said Norman Sterner, in a deep, gruff voice.

"I don't know what you're talking about," said Mitzi. "The Tannery is closed. You'll have to leave."

"You know what's been hidden in here," said Sterner, brandishing a gun. "Don't pretend you don't know what I mean. Hand it over, or this time, there might just be two bodies found in the vat."

Her heart pounding, Adele took a step back, just as she saw the door move behind Sterner. A bloodied hand reached around the door, pushing it hard against Sterner's back. Adele screamed, or rather, made a noise that sounded more like, "Aaaaaaak!" Not exactly the delicate shriek of a damsel in distress, but effective nonetheless.

Sterner was startled, quickly turned around and saw a man standing in the doorway. Stuffing the gun in his slicker pocket, he ran across the stone floor and out the back door that led to the road and stone-arched bridge across the Monocacy Creek.

"Hey Adele, could you take me to the ER?" asked Zeke, standing there in the doorway, sweaty and injured, oblivious to the little drama he had stumbled into. "Some guy elbowed me in the eye and I think I might need stitches."

"Did you see what just happened here?" asked Adele in total shock. "That man tried to kill us!"

"What?" Zeke answered. "I couldn't see a thing with all of the blood in my face. Could we go now, hon? I want to get fixed up so I can get home and watch the game on TV tonight."

"Unbelievable," said Adele, shaking her head. "This is why I don't like to leave him unsupervised." Turning to Mitzi, she said, "I hope you have your cell phone with you. We have to call the police right away."

"I've already called the police. They are on their way. I'm trying to get my staff over here to help us. I'm calling now," said Mitzi, her phone to her ear.

"Good," said Adele. "I've got to get Zeke to the ER."

The police arrived quickly and Mitzi was able to explain what happened. Officers started searching the grounds, but Sterner was long gone.

Mitzi pulled the tin box out from its hiding place and gave it to the officer who was questioning her.

"I would appreciate it if you don't make the contents of this box public when you do your report," she said. "I don't want people breaking in and looking for more treasure."

The officer said that he would do what he could. Mitzi and her staff locked up the Tannery and returned to the Old Mill. Finally back in the safety of her own office, she took a deep breath, notified her board, and began to write up one of the strangest incident reports she'd ever written.

CHAPTER FOURTEEN

To Catch a Thief

T HE next morning, Mitzi sat reading the newspaper at her kitchen table as Vaughn made tea for both of them. Even though they subscribed to several newspapers online, she enjoyed reading the actual physical newspaper and holding it in her hands.

She was pleased to see that the police officer was able to comply with her request. The small article in the newspaper simply said that there was an attempted robbery in the Industrial Quarter.

"Did you get in touch with Mark Sargent yet?" Vaughn asked, pouring hot water into their mugs.

"I was able to leave a voice message. I asked him to call me back as soon as possible. Maybe he didn't pick up his messages last evening."

"What about Zeke? How is he doing?"

"Adele says he's fine. Just another collision on the basketball court. But thank goodness he was playing down on Sand Island and came looking for Adele when he got hurt. Who knows what Norman Sterner would have done if he hadn't been interrupted."

"I'm sure it was scary for you two," said Vaughn, "but I can't seriously imagine that he would try to hurt you over a locket, a pocket watch, and a few coins."

"When a person has a gun in his hand, and is standing right in front of you, you tend to get a little concerned," said Mitzi, her voice rising. The image of Sterner standing there in the Tannery was still fresh in her mind.

"Of course, you're right, you're right." said Vaughn. "The whole thing is just incredible. I hope the police find him soon."

Her cell phone vibrated on the table next to her. It was Mark. "Thanks for calling me back," she said, "We have to tell you what happened yesterday afternoon at the Tannery! Can you meet Adele and me at the Mill this morning? Someone threatened us and... well, we should tell you in person."

"I can come by in about twenty minutes, if that's okay. I'm just on Main Street having coffee with Beth."

"Bring her along!" said Mitzi. "She needs to hear this story, too."

Mitzi then called Adele and they decided to have Elaine and Fred join them at the Mill.

Vaughn interrupted. "What about Merrill Houser? Didn't you tell me that his great-great-great grandfather, Jedediah, was the actual culprit who started this whole incident back in 1862?"

"Of course, he should be there," conceded Mitzi.

Vaughn offered to drive Mitzi to her office at the Mill. She asked him to stay, knowing that he often added details to a story that she might have forgotten.

Adele drove the short distance from her office at the Church to the Old Mill, just as she had two weeks ago during the storm. So much has happened in such a short time, she thought. Of course, her work as a pastor hadn't stopped. After taking Zeke home from the ER, she had to return to the office last evening and had a hospital visit to make this morning. And she was scheduled to preach this Sunday, which meant that finishing her sermon had to be a priority sometime in the next 12 hours.

Ministry at Central Church was not for clergy who wanted a nice, quiet setting. Still, she had to admit that her pastorate had put her in the center of many interesting situations, although she could probably do without being threatened at gunpoint.

Beth and Mark arrived at the Mill, hand in hand, a few minutes after Adele. Shortly thereafter, the others joined the group. As the eight of them sat together in the conference room, they listened intently to Mitzi's account of what happened, starting with Radcliffe Rhoad's clues that helped Mitzi find the tin box.

"I'm so sorry that this happened to both of you," said Mark. "What a nightmare! How did this Norman Sterner know that you'd be at the Tannery yesterday?" he asked.

"He probably didn't," said Vaughn. "He was looking for the treasure and happened to walk in on Mitzi and Adele. I would think he'd be prepared to break one of the windows to get in, if necessary. But because they were already there, he didn't have to break in. The door was unlocked."

"Weren't you terrified when he threatened you with a gun?" asked Beth.

"Well, *I* was, that's for sure," said Adele. "Mitzi was able to stay cool and push the tin box back into the wall without him seeing it. And then of course my husband, with his perfect timing, interrupted him and he ran out."

"Have you heard from the police yet? Did they find him?" asked Elaine. "He could still be wandering around our streets."

"Not yet," said Mitzi.

"Did you say that they confiscated the box and the locket and pocket watch and those coins?" Mark asked.

"They did, but they said we'd be able to pick it up in about a week."

"I can't wait to see it," said Mark. "My mother often talked about the locket, especially. She wanted to see if it held actual photos of Joe and Mary."

"It does," said Mitzi. "They must have been so young when those photos were taken. I have to say that it gave me chills to see their pictures and to hold the locket and pocket watch and those coins in my hands."

"What sort of coins were they?" asked Fred, always the curious researcher. "I guess I am surprised that there wasn't paper money in the box, since the federal government was issuing paper money at that point."

"I know," said Mitzi. "We have a few paper bills from the time of the Civil War in our collection. I didn't really expect to see gold coins, either."

During this whole discussion, Merrill sat pensively, head lowered, not looking at anyone.

Mitzi got up from her chair and asked them to follow her over to the Tannery to see the hiding place. They tried to imagine how Joe hid the box, but was interrupted by his killer on that fateful night in 1862.

"Joe Carver was in such a panicked state that he had to act quickly," said Mitzi. "His letter to Mary reveals that he must have shared his concerns with the pastor of Central Church, trusting the pastor to post the letter and help Mary find her way to the Tannery. But he never told Mary how to find the box with its treasures."

After another half hour of speculating, they decided to be on their way, but to stay in touch if the police came up with any leads. Mitzi lingered in the Tannery.

As she turned, Merrill was still there as well. The morning shadows cast a cold, discomforting chill throughout the old stone-walled Tannery.

"What is it?" asked Mitzi, hesitantly.

In a voice barely above a whisper, Merrill said, "All of this about Joe Carver and the watch, the locket and the coins and the murder. Is it possible that Jedediah, my own ancestor, was responsible for this tragedy? It's almost more than I can bear."

He turned, opened the heavy wooden door and walked out.

Mitzi stood there in the stillness of the moment. She never would have guessed that the story of Joe Carver would affect Merrill so dramatically. What other mysteries lie hidden in these walls, she wondered, suddenly feeling transported back to the crime scene long ago. Did Jedediah really murder Joe? We may never know.

All of a sudden, the door swung open again, this time, to the cheerful voices of twenty-three cub scouts on the first tour of the day.

Within 24 hours, the police called Mitzi to tell her that Norman Sterner had been apprehended. But his name wasn't really Norman Sterner. It was none other than Warren Pritchard, the antiques dealer from the Poconos who had befriended Mark Sargent's mother. He was wanted in Cumberland County for the theft of historical documents. The warrant for his arrest was enough for the police to detain him, not to mention the fact that he didn't have a permit to carry a weapon.

As word got out about the Tannery incident and the Joe and Mary Carver story, the number of visitors to the Industrial Quarter increased. Mitzi had to hire another few docents to guide people through the reopened Tannery. With Mark's enthusiastic agreement, she decided to display the locket and pocket watch in a place of honor in the Moravian Museum, along with a printed narrative about the Carver family.

Baxter Hemphill was thrilled to banter with the flood of Civil War buffs and re-enactors who stopped in the Church office every few days to ask directions to the Tannery. Baxter never discussed, with anyone, who it was who let Norman Sterner into the Church office that Sunday morning. Let it just be one of those unsolved mysteries, he thought.

When Merrill Houser heard about the display in the Museum, he actually had very little to say. Merrill seemed less combative lately, cooperative even. Although perplexed by this change in his behavior, Mitzi went against her researcher instincts and didn't ask questions; she just enjoyed the respite from his bad behavior.

Even after Mark Sargent learned what he'd come to Bethlehem to find out, he now found many good reasons to come back to Bethlehem. Most of them had to do with the lovely Beth Ettwein.

After this stressful episode, Beth decided to move back to town to be with her mother. Elaine, of course, treated Mark like family. They found a lot in common, after all. Elaine was keeper of her family history, just as Mark's mother had been keeper of the Carver family history.

CHAPTER FIFTEEN

A Wedding at Moravian Days

M ORAVIAN Days opened on a clear, cool morning the following June. Mitzi and Adele had watched with amazement over the months as the plans they had made came to life through the work of all the volunteers who stepped forward to help.

There were large white canopy tents scattered under the trees around the Church Green. Picnic tables were set for everyone to enjoy hot dogs and hamburgers from the grill, along with baked potatoes and corn on the cob.

The Bethlehem Area Moravians' Trombone Choir played chorales from the belfry of Central Moravian Church as Historical Society docents in 18th century Moravian garb, both the women in their long colonial dresses with white *haubes* on their heads and the men dressed in shirts and vests and knee breeches, chatted with visitors who walked up the steps from Main Street.

And just to confirm that all was right with the world, their favorite, iconic little Nazareth bakery supplied large sheets of delicious Moravian sugar cake for the crowds to sample. It was a staple at all Moravian events, loaded with lots of sugar and butter and its long history in the church.

Over the next two days, there were lectures in the Old Chapel about Moravian life and beliefs and first person presentations from actors portraying prominent Moravian leaders over the years. Inside the Christian Education Building, there were displays of Moravian handi-work, photos of the mission work of local Moravian churches and a large multi-paneled timeline of Moravian history, prepared by the Moravian Archives in honor of the 250th anniversary of Moravians in Bethlehem.

Next to the Old Chapel, people were coming and going from the Moravian Museum to see exhibits highlighting life in Bethlehem in the 1700's.

At the far end of the Church Green, the Kemerer Museum displayed maps of how Bethlehem changed from a small Moravian enclave to the city it was today. And in God's Acre, the historic cemetery on the campus, Junior Docents were giving tours, pointing out the grave markers, dating back to 1742. People were especially interested in finding the grave stone of Joe Carver.

But probably the most touching event of Moravian Days was the wedding of a couple in the Old Chapel. Although warned to expect many visitors to be stopping in or observing them taking their wedding photos on the Green, the couple was thrilled to be married right in the midst of all the festivities.

As always, the 1751 Old Chapel was beautiful in the simplicity of its white walls and large windows with their wide sills. White beeswax candles flickered in the pewter sconces along the walls. As the officiating pastor, Adele gathered with the groom and male attendants in the Minister's Room at the back of the Chapel, while the female sacristans fussed over the bride and her bridesmaids downstairs in the Bride's Room.

Adele, dressed in the traditional Moravian surplice, took her place up front.

The newly renovated Chapel organ sounded glorious as the prelude began. The wedding service itself was simple and traditional and was embellished today with special music and the exchanging of vows that the couple had written.

After Adele pronounced the benediction and introduced the couple for the first time, the bride and groom led the procession out to the broad, red brick walkway to receive their guests. The tourists gathered on the Green for Moravian Days joined in the shouts of celebration as the couple appeared on the steps at the front door of the Old Chapel.

The congregation flowed out onto the Green and two young people stepped apart from the crowd to share a moment together.

"Well, Mark and Beth, now you've seen how it's done," grinned Vaughn, spying them sharing a kiss. "Maybe you two will be next!"

"My mom looks so beautiful doesn't she?" said Beth, blushing a bit and holding onto Mark's arm.

"She and Merrill make a wonderful couple," said Mitzi, still somewhat in shock that Elaine and Merrill had found each other. It certainly explained a lot about Merrill's more mellow behavior lately.

Finally, Adele emerged from the Chapel and stood at the steps, looking out at the wedding party and the people surrounding them. From a distance, she caught Mitzi's eye as both women smiled and nodded in approval at a wonderful conclusion to Moravian Days.

"There's just one thing I need to tell you," said Vaughn, as he and Mitzi walked arm and arm across the Green and toward the Hotel for the wedding reception.

"Oh, what's that?" asked Mitzi, eying him suspiciously, thinking that he was going to say that he forgot to send over their wedding gift.

"You know the brown canvas pouch that you found in the tin box at the Tannery?"

"Yes…?"

"You may not have noticed it, but take a closer look next time you see it. There is a faint inscription on the bag that says, 'Paymaster, US Army.' "

"What does that mean?" Mitzi asked, stopping on the sidewalk to face him.

"It means that maybe 'Norman Sterner' or 'Warren Pritchard' or whatever his name is, may have had the hunch that if Jedediah Houser were the paymaster for his unit, there may have been more than a few coins involved. Perhaps Jedediah gambled away the whole payroll for the new recruits. Joe Carver may have won big at cards and stashed a whole lot more than what you found in the bag. Maybe the real treasure is still hidden somewhere in the Tannery."

"Oh my," said Mitzi, dismayed at the thought of more Norman Sterners or Warren Pritchards sniffing around the Tannery.

"Maybe I'll just forget that you said that, at least for this evening."

"Good idea," said Vaughn as they started across Main Street to the celebration at Hotel B.

A Glossary of Moravian Terms

Choir system - A form of communal living in early Bethlehem in which members of a particular group resided, worked and worshipped together. Single Sisters, for example, lived in the Single Sisters' House, independent of their families.

Christmas Putz - From the German word, *putzen*, meaning to clean or to decorate, a Putz depicts the story of the birth of Jesus through miniature Putz figures arranged in various biblical scenes.

Haube - A traditional form-fitting white head covering worn by Moravian women in the 1700's to the mid 1800's. Also called a Schneppelhaube, (*Schneppel* meaning 'beak,') it featured a beak-like point at the forehead.

Polly Heckewelder doll - "Polly" is remembered as the first white child born in the Ohio territories in 1781. Her father was John Heckewelder, noted Moravian missionary to the Native Americans. Members of a Native American tribe made the first Polly doll in 1782. The fabric doll that was later created for sale in her honor in 1872, was of a little girl of the time, clad in a blue or pink gingham dress and white pinafore. The Ladies' Sewing Society, formed in 1861, sews the Polly dolls today and sells them for the benefit of Moravian causes.

Surplice - A white robe worn by Moravian clergy for baptism and for the service of Holy Communion. It is also worn for the celebration of marriage.

Tannery - A tannery is a place where animal hides are processed into leather. The Tannery was constructed in 1761 and is located in the Colonial Industrial Quarter next to the butchery to tan hides into leather. Moravian tanners produced about 3,000 hides a year for use by the community and as a product to raise funds to support the community. Although the Moravian Church sold the tannery and its operations in 1830, tanning continued until the building was converted into a multi-family residence in 1873. The building was restored 1968-1971; an archaeological report, pieces of the original vats, and tools are in the Historic Bethlehem Museums & Sites collection.

Historic Bethlehem Museums & Sites

HISTORIC Bethlehem Museums & Sites (HBMS) is a 501(c)(3) nonprofit organization that formed in 1993 to consolidate the operations of several local museums and historic sites. Historic Bethlehem Museums & Sites interprets three centuries of the history and culture of Bethlehem from its founding as a Moravian community in 1741 to the 21st century through tours, exhibits and programs.

Historic Bethlehem Museums & Sites maintains 20 historic buildings and sites in Bethlehem.

The Moravian Museum of Bethlehem includes the 1741 Gemeinhaus, the 1752 Apothecary and herb garden, the 1744/1752 Single Sisters' House, and the 1758/1765 Nain-Schober House.

The Colonial Industrial Quarter, America's earliest industrial park situated on a 10 acre site, includes the 1762 Waterworks, the 1761 Tannery, 1750 Smithy (reconstructed), 1780/1830 Miller's House, 1869 Luckenbach Mill, 1750s Springhouse (reconstructed), and the archeological remains of the 1740s Pottery, 1770s Dye House, 1750s Butchery, and 1700s Oil Mill.

The 1810 Goundie House and Visitor Center is housed in the 1830s Schropp Shop on Main Street.

The 1748/1848 Burnside Plantation, a 6.5 acre farm in the city, includes the 1748/1818 farmhouse, 1820s summer kitchen and corncrib, 1840s wagon shed and two 1840s bank barns, one with the only operating high horse-powered wheel in the U.S., a kitchen garden, an apple orchard, and two meadows.

The Kemerer Museum of Decorative Arts, housed in three interconnected mid-1800s homes, features changing exhibits, period rooms, and galleries with furniture, paintings, china, clothing, silver and doll house collection highlighting over three centuries of decorative arts. This museum speaks to the changes in style and design over the years.

HBMS has over 60,000 artifacts in its combined collections. In addition, the HBMS Library and Archives has 10,000 photographs, thousands of documents, letters, maps related to the history of Bethlehem, and a 2,000 volume library.

In 2003, Historic Bethlehem Museums & Sites became a founding member of the International Moravian Heritage Network, one of six key 18th century historic Moravian communities worldwide.

In 2004, HBMS was named an affiliate of the Smithsonian Institution, one of only 180 museums in the United States to receive this honor.

Website: www.historicbethlehem.org

Historic Moravian Bethlehem

IN 2012, Historic Moravian Bethlehem was designated a National Historic Landmark District by the U.S. Secretary of the Interior. It encompasses just over 14 acres in the heart of the City of Bethlehem within the Central Bethlehem National Register Historic District.

It was here in 1741 at the confluence of the Monocacy Creek and the Lehigh River that the first Moravians felled white oak trees and began building their community on a 500 acre tract purchased in the spring. They located their crafts, trades, and industries along the waterways and their institutional dwellings on the limestone bluff above.

The earliest structures were built of hewn logs. The first house is no longer extant; however, the second structure known as the 1741 Gemein-haus (National Historic Landmark) is still standing and houses the Moravian Museum of Bethlehem. A majority of the 18th century German Colonial style stone structures remain including the 1744-1772 Bell House/Sisters' House Complex, 1748 Single Brethren's House, 1751 Old Chapel, 1761 Tannery, 1762 Waterworks (National Historic Landmark), 1768 Widows' House, 1782-1834 Miller's House, and the archeological remains of the butchery, dye house, pottery, and oil mill. In the center of the District is the 1803-1806 Central Moravian Church built in the Federal style. A contributing property to the District is the 1810 Goundie House, one of the earliest brick homes in the Federal architectural style.

The Moravians in Bethlehem lived in a communal society organized into groups, called choirs, segregated by age, gender, and marital status. The society also operated under a General Economy where everyone worked for the good of the community and received care from cradle to grave. Based on their societal organization, the community developed large institutional choir houses, superb examples of German Colonial style architecture in America.

Historic Moravian Bethlehem encompasses excellent examples of the architecture and town planning of the 18th century community. Today, a Moravian from the mid-1700s would recognize their community and feel at home walking the streets of this part of the City of Bethlehem. Many of these buildings have been in continuous use since they were constructed and some for their original purpose.

Central Moravian Church

Bethlehem was founded by members of the Moravian Church and named on December 24, 1741, by their leader Count Nicholas Ludwig von Zinzendorf. As the early community outgrew its worship spaces, the 1741 Gemeinhaus Saal, as well as the 1751 Old Chapel, a third place of worship was needed. Central Moravian Church was built between 1803 and 1806 to accommodate 1,500 people at a time when the total population of Bethlehem was only 580. Today, the seating capacity is 1,100.

Without interior pillars, the heavy roof and belfry are supported by 68-foot-long white oak timbers whose ends rest on the side walls rising from massive foundations. From the iconic belfry, the Bethlehem Area Moravians' Trombone Choir, the oldest brass choir in continuous existence in the United States, announces the deaths of members of the congregation, as well as festivals of the church and community. The belfry houses the oldest working American-made tower clock, built in Bethlehem in 1747. The current bell was hung in 1868.

The Moravians brought an outstanding musical culture with them to America, and Central Moravian Church became known as one of the most prestigious places for music. Haydn's oratorio, *The Creation*, was performed for the first time in America in Central Moravian Church in 1811. The first American performance of Bach's complete *Mass in B Minor* was also held in Central Moravian Church in 1900. The latter earned the church status as a National Landmark of Music. USA Today, December 18, 1998, named Central Moravian Church one of the nation's "Ten Great Places to Reflect on Christmas Eve."

Through the years, Central Moravian Church has been the spiritual home of noteworthy musicians, scientists, craftspeople, writers, poets, artists, physicians, educators, and civic leaders. Today, worship services are held on Sundays at 9 a.m. in the Old Chapel and at 11 a.m. in the Sanctuary. Summer worship (June-August) is at 10 a.m.

Website: www.centralmoravianchurch.org

Moravian Denomination

THE Moravian Church had its origin in the pre-Reformation awakening under Jan Hus. The Church was organized formally as the *Unitas Fratrum*, the Unity of the Brethren, in 1457. Because much of its early history centered in Moravia, now part of the Czech Republic, the Unity became known as the Moravian Church. The Moravian Church was renewed in Herrnhut, Germany, in 1727, and is recognized as one of the oldest organized Protestant denominations in the world.

The Old Moravian Chapel

THE Old Moravian Chapel was constructed in 1751 as the second place of worship for the Moravian Congregation of Bethlehem. Originally, the Chapel could be entered only from the Gemeinhaus and Bell House, with the men and women entering through separate doors. The Communion Table (pulpit area) was on the west wall instead of the south wall as it is today. In 1865, the Chapel was altered and an entrance was added on the north wall.

Many notable people worshiped in the Chapel during the Revolutionary War period, including Benjamin Franklin, Martha Washington, George Washington; also John Adams, Samuel Adams, Marquis de Lafayette, John Hancock, Ethan Allen, Count Casimir Pulaski, General Horatio Gates and John Paul Jones.

On March 10, 1792, fifty one chiefs and representatives of the Six-Nations (Iroquois Confederacy) came to Bethlehem on their way to Philadelphia to meet with George Washington. Among them were the great chiefs Red Jacket, Corn Planter and Big Tree. They gathered in the Chapel, the Indians in ceremonial feathers and leggings and the brethren and sisters in their plain garb.

The Old Chapel is used for early worship on Sunday, weddings, funerals and special musical programs during Advent and Lent. Moravian Academy uses the Chapel for weekly services and other special events.

The Moravian Archives

THE Moravian Archives is the official repository for the records of the Moravian Church in America - Northern Province. The Northern Province covers the Moravian churches in the United States (except for North Carolina, Florida, Georgia and Virginia) and Canada. Records from the Moravian Church in Alaska, Labrador, Nicaragua and the Eastern West-Indies can also be found in the Archives.

Located in a modern 9,200 square foot building with two climate-controlled vaults, the Moravian Archives contains approximately 8,000 linear feet of material.

Documents stored in the Archives provide the history of the province beginning in 1740 and include records of many congregations. There are over 1,000,000 pages written in 18th-century German script, large numbers of English-language documents, over 20,000 printed volumes and thousands of pamphlets, paintings, prints, maps, and photographs as well as selected personal papers.

The Archives is open Monday through Friday, 8 a.m. to 4:30 p.m.

Website: www.moravianchurcharchives.org

Bethlehem Area Moravians, Inc.

BETHLEHEM Area Moravians, Inc., had its beginnings in the old Moravian Congregation of Bethlehem. The original Congregation was comprised of three local churches: Central, College Hill and West Side Moravian Churches. At one point, Edgeboro Moravian Church was also a part of the Congregation.

Together, members of the Congregation gathered to celebrate Christmas Eve, Children's Lovefeast in September, Easter Dawn and the Anniversary of the founding of the Congregation on June 25, 1742. The organization was governed by a General Board of Elders and a General Board of Trustees, whose responsibilities paralleled that of individual church boards.

During the 250th anniversary year of 1992, Bethlehem Area Moravians, Inc. was formed and now includes Central, College Hill, West Side, Edgeboro, East Hills and Advent Moravian Churches. "BAM" serves and ministers to people in the Bethlehem community, especially through housing. A number of Moravian Houses have been developed for those who qualify because of particular needs.

Moravian Village, a continuing care retirement community sponsored by BAM, provides comfortable and secure living for older adults.

Moravian College Housing, also known as the HILL, is a living and learning residence for 231 Moravian College students. This facility is sponsored by BAM and provides a comfortable, safe and superior learning environment.

For Further Reading

Caldwell, Douglas W. and Reifinger, Carol A. *Let Us Go Over to Bethlehem: A Guide to the Moravian Community.* Bethlehem, PA: Central Moravian Church, 2007.

Hamilton, Kenneth G. *Church Street in Old Bethlehem.* Bethlehem, PA: Moravian Congregation of Bethlehem, 1988.

Howland, Garth A. *An Architectural History of the Moravian Church.* Bethlehem, PA: Times Publishing Co., 1947.

Huetter, Karen Zerbe. *The Bethlehem Waterworks.* Bethlehem, PA: Historic Bethlehem, Inc., 1976.

LeCount, Charles A. *The Blacksmiths of Early Bethlehem.* Bethlehem, PA: 1992.

Levering, Joseph Mortimer. *A History of Bethlehem, Pennsylvania 1741-1892.* Bethlehem, PA: Times Publishing Company, 1903.

Nelson, Vernon H. *The Bethlehem Gemeinhaus.* Bethlehem, PA: Moravian Congregation of Bethlehem, 1990.

Schwarz, Ralph Grayson. *Bethlehem on the Lehigh.* Bethlehem, PA: Bethlehem Area Foundation, 1991.

Sweitzer, Vangie Roby. *Christmas In Bethlehem: A Moravian Heritage.* Bethlehem, PA: Central Moravian Church, 2000.

—. *The Moravian Christmas Putz.* Bethlehem, PA: Central Moravian Church, 2013.

—. *Tuned for Praise: The Bethlehem Area Moravian Trombone Choir,* 1754-2004. Bethlehem, PA: Central Moravian Church, 2004.

Visit, Explore, Experience Historic Moravian Bethlehem,Pennsylvania. Bethlehem, PA: Historic Bethlehem Museums & Sites, 2014.

Zug, Jeanette Barres. *The Old Moravian Chapel.* Bethlehem, PA: 1989.

About the Authors

CHARLENE DONCHEZ MOWERS is President of Historic Bethlehem Museums & Sites. A native of Bethlehem, she has been involved in preserving and interpreting the history of this community for over 20 years. She serves on the Discover Lehigh Valley Board of Directors and the Bethlehem Council of the Greater Lehigh Valley Chamber of Commerce. She served as co-chair of the Lehigh Valley Industrial Heritage Coalition and is a representative to the International Moravian Heritage Network. She chairs the Archives Committee of Moravian Academy. She has been a guest speaker at preservation and museum-related conferences, including the Pennsylvania Federation of Museums and Historical Organizations, Preservation Pennsylvania, Smithsonian Institution, and the international Moravian Heritage Network Conferences.

Previously, she chaired the Bethlehem Tourism Authority Board, served on the Chistkindlmarkt Council and the Board of Trustees of Moravian Academy, and was a library volunteer at the Allentown Art Museum.

She has a B.A. from Arcadia University and an M.A. from Temple University. She is a Distinguished Alumna of Moravian Academy. She and her husband reside in Bethlehem.

CAROL A. REIFINGER retired as Senior Pastor of Central Moravian Church after twenty-eight years in ministry. She received her Master of Divinity Degree from Moravian Theological Seminary in 1984.

As a Pastor of Central Moravian Church, she served Bethlehem Area Moravians, Inc., from its inception, as an Executive Board member, as Vice President, and as Ministries Committee Chair. Part of her work with the Board was to develop the Moravian Village Continuing Care Retirement Community, which was sponsored by Bethlehem Area Moravians, Inc.

Excerpts from *The Body in the Vat:*

"His heart pounded as the footsteps came closer. Suddenly, the door to the hall swung open and a shot exploded at his head."

———

"Adele glanced at the clock on her desk and then out the window and realized that it wasn't just getting to be evening, but the skies had darkened with storm clouds."

———

"The Old Mill looked especially foreboding tonight because the office windows on the first floor were completely dark, but a pale yellow light was still shining out into the parking lot from Mitzi's office on the second floor."

———

"As the stranger left, Adele closed the door behind him, wondering how he'd managed to get in the office."

———

"As Mitzi left her office to walk across the grounds to the Tannery, she felt a tinge of uneasiness."

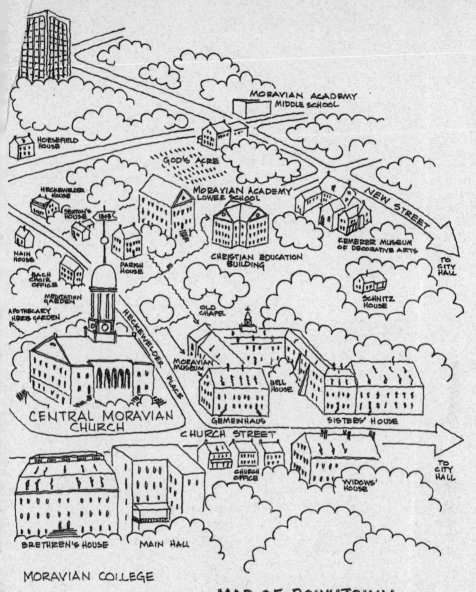

MORAVIAN ACADEMY
MIDDLE SCHOOL

HORSEFIELD
HOUSE

GOD'S ACRE

HECKEWELDER
HOUSE

SEXTON'S
HOUSE

1803

MORAVIAN ACADEMY
LOWER SCHOOL

NEW STREET

NAIN
HOUSE

BACH
CHOIR
OFFICE

PARISH
HOUSE

CHRISTIAN EDUCATION
BUILDING

KEMERER MUSEUM
OF DECORATIVE ARTS

TO
CITY
HALL

MEDITATION
GARDEN

APOTHECARY
HERB GARDEN

OLD
CHAPEL

SCHNITZ
HOUSE

HECKEWELDER PLACE

MORAVIAN
MUSEUM

BELL
HOUSE

CENTRAL MORAVIAN
CHURCH

GEMEINHAUS

SISTERS' HOUSE

CHURCH STREET

TO
CITY
HALL

CHURCH
OFFICE

WIDOWS'
HOUSE

BRETHREN'S HOUSE

MAIN HALL

MORAVIAN COLLEGE

MAP OF DOWNTOWN

BETHLEHEM

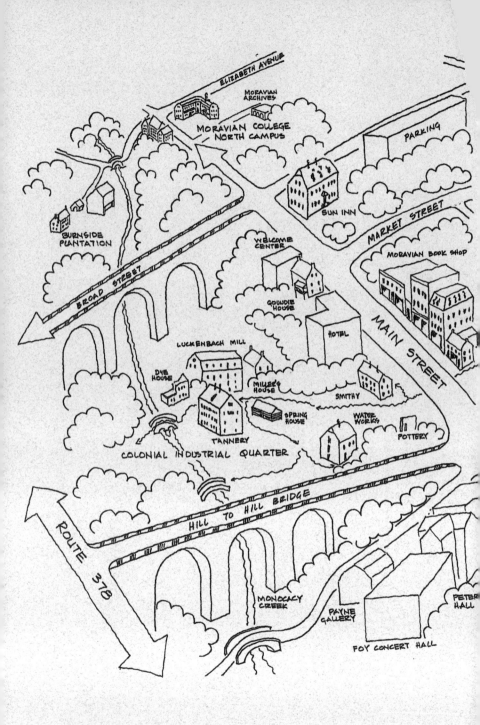

The Body in the Vat
Tales from the Tannery

Map of Bethlehem
Including the
Colonial Industrial Quarter

She co-authored the book, *Let Us Go Over to Bethlehem, A Guide to the Moravian Community,* with her former colleague, the late Rev. Dr. Douglas W. Caldwell.

She is enjoying a busy retirement as a volunteer at the Moravian Archives and as Manager of Central Church's Star and Candle Shoppe. She lives in Bethlehem with her husband, Jim.